*for Rosemary*

# THE HUNTER
# AND THE ANIMALS

*Tomie dePaola 1987*

# The Hunter and the Animals

A WORDLESS PICTURE BOOK

by Tomie de Paola

Holiday House, New York

*Library of Congress Cataloging in Publication Data*

De Paola, Tomie.
The hunter and the animals.

Summary: When the discouraged hunter falls
asleep, the forest animals play a trick on him.
[1. Hunting—Fiction.  2. Forest animals—
Fiction.  3. Stories without words]  I. Title.
PZ7.D439Hu          [E]          81-2875
ISBN 0-8234-0397-1                    AACR2
ISBN 0-8234-0428-5 (pbk.)

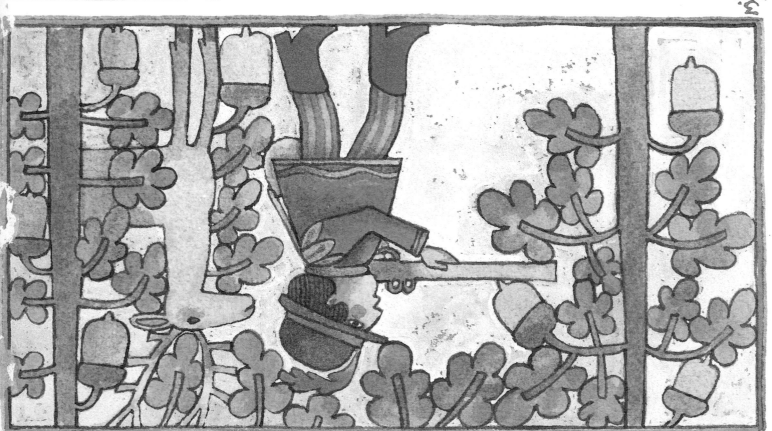

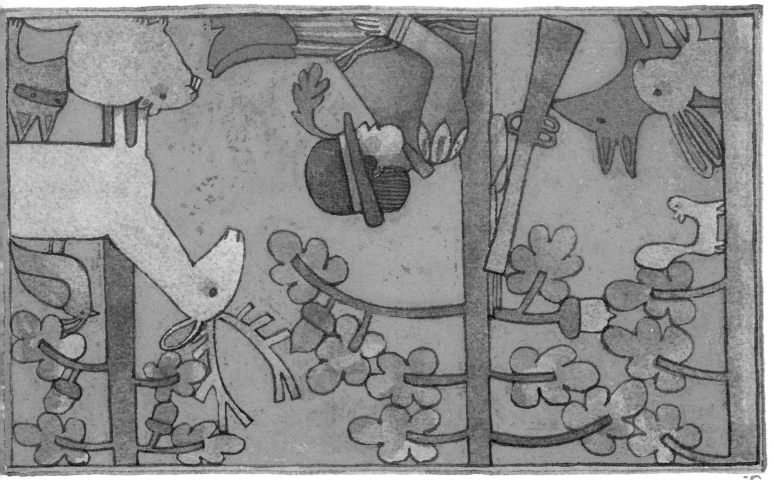

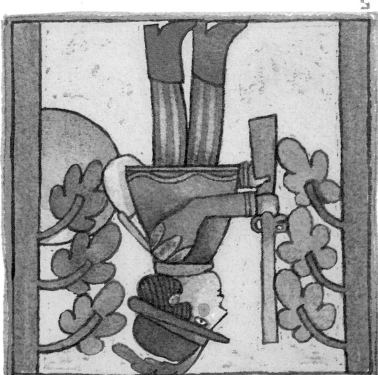

3.

4.

6.

1.

2.

3.

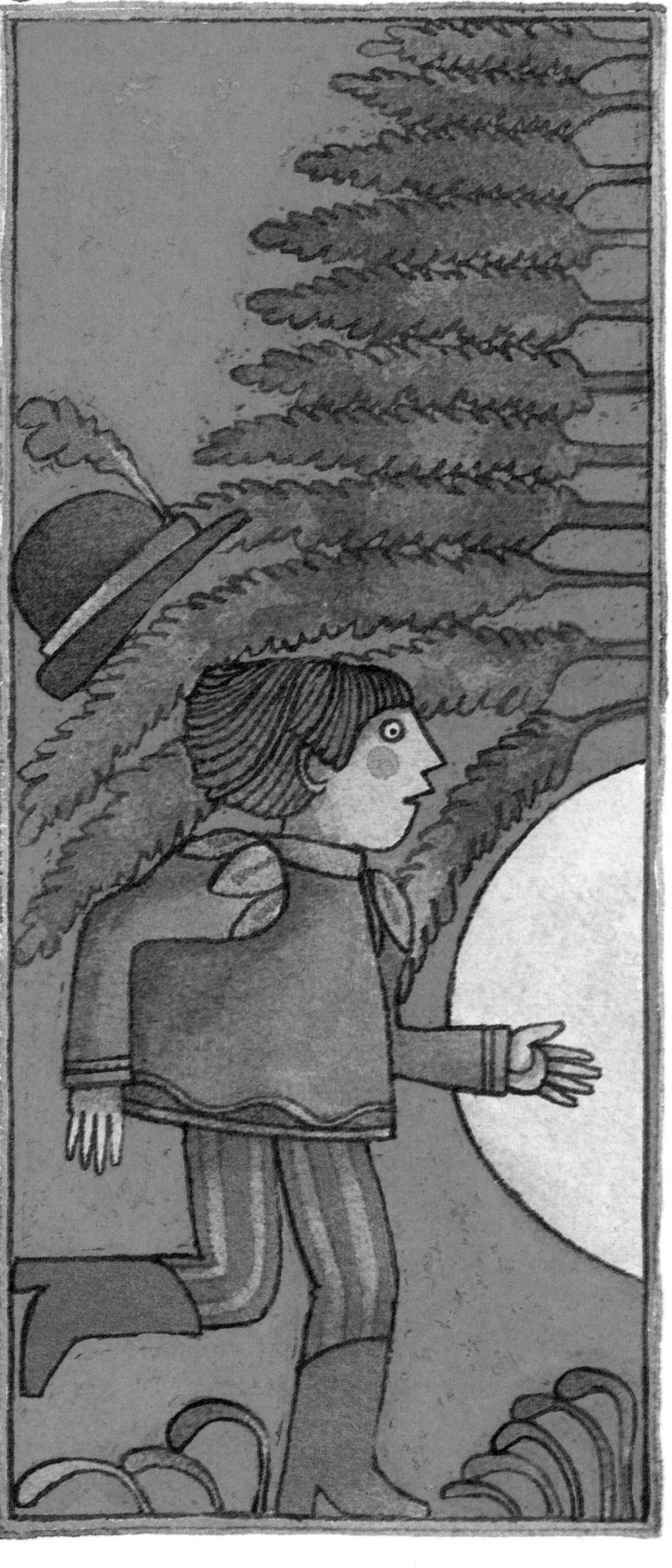

4.

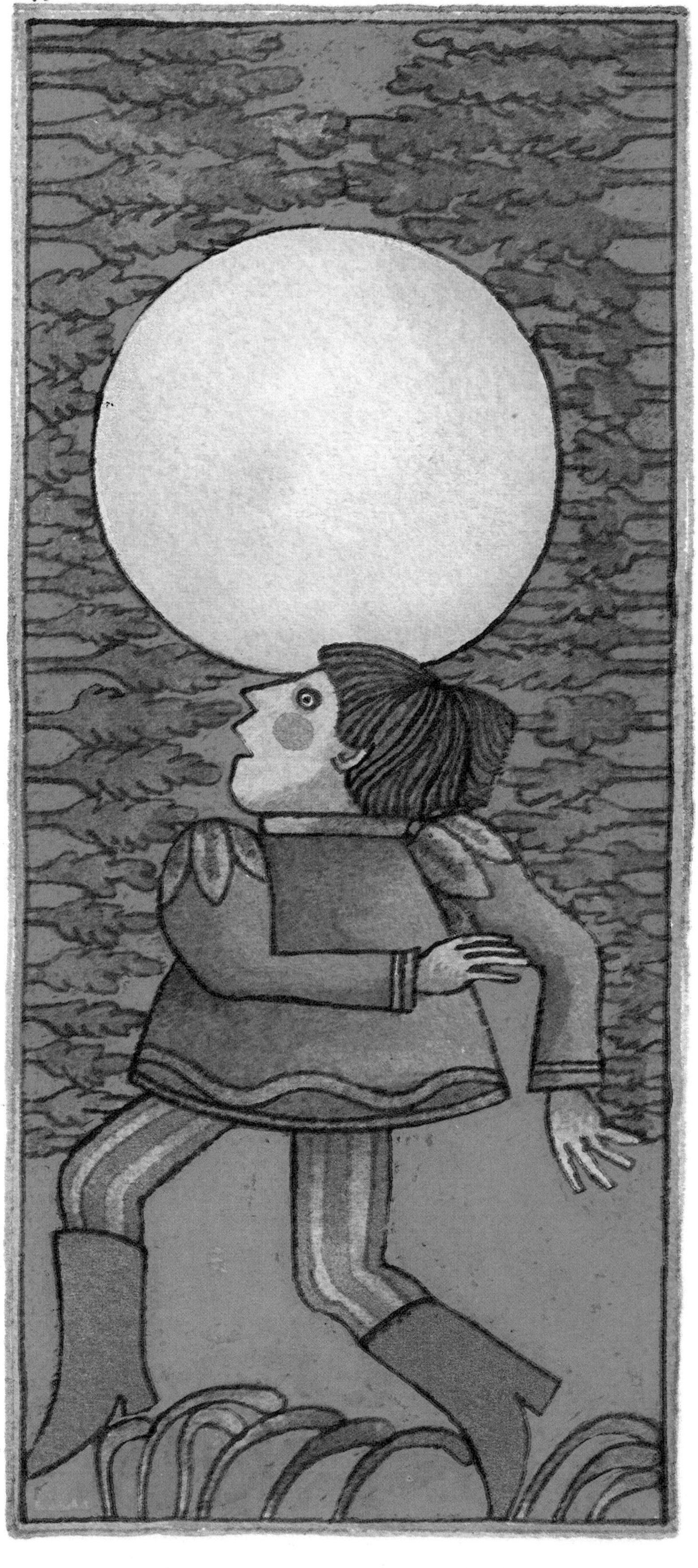

**1.**

**2.**

**5.**

1.

2.

3.

## ABOUT THIS BOOK

While looking through the volume, *Hungarian Folk Art* by Tamas Hofer and Edit Fel, Tomie de Paola came across a cut-out painted wood panel showing a hunter with two rabbits sitting by his feet and a fox climbing down a tree behind him. The picture had so much charm that Mr. de Paola decided to create a story around it—and that was the beginning of *The Hunter and the Animals.*

To capture the unique quality of Hungarian folk art, the artist made careful use of negative space. He dry-brushed opaque tempera paint onto the background so little pieces of the color underneath showed through. He drew his images in a heavy brown-black line and used transparent colored inks to emphasize the many connecting shapes that determined the negative space of the background.

The art was prepared on 140-lb. rough handmade Fabriano watercolor paper. Color separations were made by Capper, Inc. The book was printed by offset on 80-lb. Moistrite Matte by Rae Publishing Co. and bound by A. Horowitz & Sons.